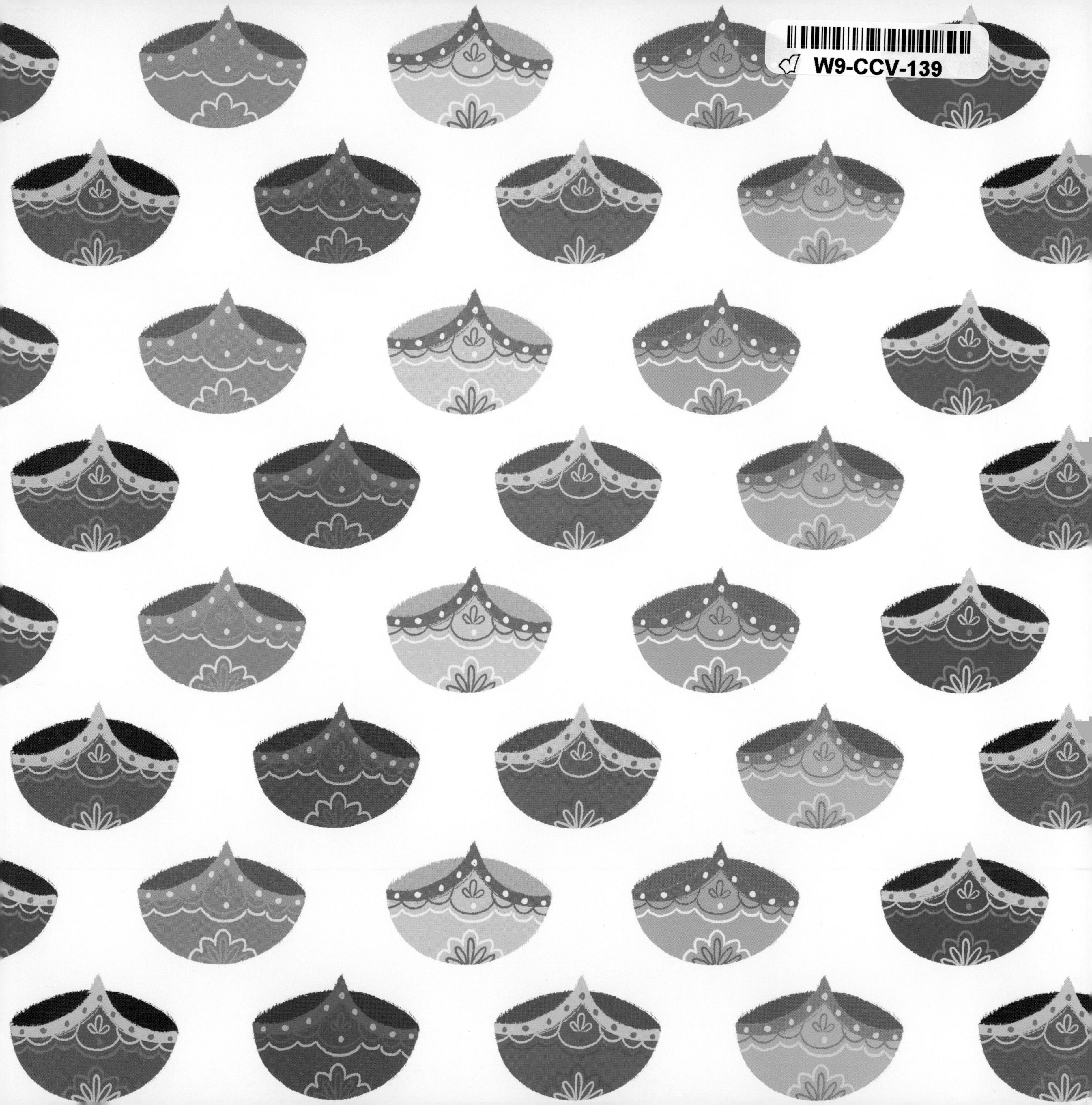

BINNY'S

BY THRITY UMRIGAR

ILLUSTRATIONS BY NIDHI CHANANI

SCHOLASTIC PRESS / NEW YORK • AN IMPRINT OF SCHOLASTIC INC.

DIWALI

Binny woke up happy but nervous. It was her day to share about Diwali, the Festival of Lights!

Since her class was learning about different celebrations, her teacher, Mr. Boomer, had asked her to talk about her favorite holiday.

Last month, Sara talked about Rosh Hashanah. And today, it was Binny's turn. She hoped everything would go just as she and her teacher had planned.

Biome
Animals

Binny started getting ready for school. She smiled as she noticed the Indian outfit Mom and Dad had laid on her chair. Maybe it was the perfect day to wear her new blue suede shoes, for good luck.

Binny turned around and got a glimpse of her mom looking so beautiful in the bright red silk sari Dad had bought her for Diwali.

Everybody went shopping for Diwali — kids got new clothes and toys, parents bought each other jewelry, and friends exchanged gift baskets filled with cakes and sweets and nuts.

SARI PALACE
Little India Bazaar

Wearing her new clothes, Binny ran downstairs for breakfast. Instead of cereal, Mom and Dad had a treat for her: warm *jalebis*, orange discs of sweetness that melted in her mouth when she bit into them. And soft, milky *pedas* that crumbled in her mouth and made her lick her lips.

Dad quickly packed the rest for her class. "May the words you speak today be as sweet as *jalebis* and as soft as *pedas*," he said.

Mom drove Binny to school.

"Remember to tell them about the oil lamps," she told Binny as she kissed her goodbye. "Good luck, Bin. You will do great."

After morning circle time, Mr. Boomer called Binny's name.

But when she stood before the class a terrible thing began to happen. Suddenly she felt so shy and scared, her mind went blank.

Some children began to giggle. Others fidgeted, not knowing what to do.

"Today is Diwali . . ." Binny said nervously.

"Diwa — WHO?" yelled Tommy.

The teacher stood up and gave the sign for quiet.

Binny *did* want to share her favorite holiday with her friends. But she couldn't find the words.

Mr. Boomer put a kindly hand on her shoulder. "Take a deep breath," he whispered. "I know you can do this."

Just then, Binny remembered what Mom had told her about the lamps:

To celebrate Diwali, people lit little oil lamps, called *diyas*, and put them by their front doors to guide good luck into their homes and chase away the darkness.

All over the world, Diwali marked the victory of goodness and light.

Binny now knew what to say: "Diwali is the Festival of Lights! It is a Hindu holiday that lasts five days and it celebrates the victory of goodness and hope!"

She told them about the fireworks, how they whistled through the air and burst like stars in the night sky, leaving streaks of gold and red and green.

She described the sparklers Dad lit in the yard, how she made figure eights with them, the golden sparks opening like a flower.

Mr. Boomer brought over the streamers that Binny had made. She took out some colorful glitter and asked Juliet and Aisha to help her make them brighter.

The class gathered around Mr. Boomer's desk as Binny handed him a tiny electric clay *diya*.

The teacher turned it on. The small flickering light looked so pretty that all the children oohed and aahed.

Binny told them that if, on Diwali, you looked down from an airplane, you'd see the city shine like a diamond, lights shimmering everywhere you looked.

She made them close their eyes and imagine a dark sky with a million twinkling stars. Diwali is a magical time for children everywhere.

Binny had one more thing to show them, the best thing of all:

She took out bags of colored powder (red, blue, yellow, purple, green, and orange), and sprinkled them onto the floor. First, she drew a flower with the powdered chalk. Then she used it to write:

HAPPY DIWALI TO ALL

HAPPY
DIWALI
TO ALL

The children started clapping. Binny went to her desk, and out came the box of *pedas* and *jalebis*, one for each student in the class. (And for Mr. Boomer, too.)

They ate every last crumb of the sweets and smacked their lips in delight.

Romeo raised his hand.

"How many festivals are there in the world?" he asked.

Binny smiled. "Thousands of them," she said. "And they are all beautiful in their own way."

Mr. Boomer leaned over to Binny and said, "Great job!"

She grinned from ear to ear.

Binny walked home that day celebrating her own victory of goodness and light.

The spirit of Diwali was real. The story of the oil lamps had chased away her own fears.

Everyone loved Diwali, this wonderful Festival of Lights.

THE DIWALI STORY

Diwali, the "Festival of Lights," marks the victory of good over evil, light over darkness. Even though it is a Hindu festival, it is celebrated by people of different faiths all across India. A national holiday in India, Diwali is also known as Deepavali, from the clay lamps (known as *diyas* or *deepas*) that people light to celebrate it.

There are many legends about why we celebrate Diwali. This is one of them:

Once upon a time, long, long ago, there lived a demon-king called Ravana. He had ten heads and twenty arms and ruled over his kingdom with cruelty and spite.

Meanwhile, the good and handsome Prince Rama had been banished from his kingdom by his wicked stepmother, who wanted her son, Bharata, to become king. Instead of arguing with her, Rama immediately gave up his crown and prepared to live a humble life in the forest. When Bharata found out what his mother had done, he begged Rama to take his rightful place on the throne. But Rama was a man of his word and he refused Bharata's pleas. Rama was accompanied by his loyal wife, Sita, and brother, Lakshmana, who also left their riches and jewels and palaces to live a simple life in the forest.

Despite having no money, Rama and Sita were in love and happy in their new, humble life. One day, Rama and Lakshmana were approached by the Wise Men and Women of the World. Ravana's demons were making their lives miserable, they complained. "We beg you to help us, O Fearless and Good Princes," they asked.

So the two good brothers went to war against Ravana's henchmen. They fought bravely and were victorious in every battle.

When word got back to Ravana he was angry as could be. In order to take revenge, he flew to the forest, kidnapped the good Princess Sita, and brought her back to his island of Lanka. After searching all over for his wife, Rama finally learned the truth about her kidnapping from Hanuman, the monkey-general. Hanuman and the other monkeys took Rama to Ravana's island to help him find his wife and bring her back home.

The battle went on for many days. On one side were the good guys: Rama, Lakshmana, Hanuman, and his band of monkeys. On the other were the bad guys: Ravana and his devious demons. At last, Rama and Ravana met in an epic battle. At first, they were evenly matched but then, finally, Rama defeated Ravana and good triumphed over evil.

People cheered all over the land and the reunion between Rama and Sita was joyful. They decided to make their way back home to Ayodhya to take their rightful place as king and queen. But they had lived away for fourteen years and so, in celebration and in gratitude, the villagers who they had helped lit lamps all along the way to help them find their way home.

Even after thousands of years, people still celebrate Diwali, the Festival of Lights, to remind us to be good and kind and brave and honest.

THE FIVE DAYS OF DIWALI

On the first day of Diwali, people often clean their homes and shop for kitchen utensils.

On the second day, homes are decorated with clay lamps and colorful patterns called *rangoli*, which are created on the floor with colored sand or powder.

On the third day, families gather to pray to the goddess Lakshmi, to enjoy a delicious feast, and to watch fireworks.

On the fourth day, friends and relatives give one another gifts and good wishes for the season.

On the fifth and last day, siblings visit one another and exchange gifts. Others use the day to clean and organize their work spaces.

We were not Hindu. But in the India in which I grew up, it didn't matter.

Everybody celebrated Diwali — Hindus, Muslims, Christians, and Zoroastrians like myself. In fact, my father was legendary for buying fireworks for all the neighborhood kids to enjoy. The younger ones like myself loved making figure eights and other patterns with our sparklers. The older, more intrepid kids were allowed to light rockets and the other firecrackers that whizzed past us on their way skyward. We loved the sound and smell and sight of these beautiful, colorful displays. At night, we'd light the small clay lamps and place them outside our apartment. And we'd make gift baskets filled with goodies to give to friends around the holiday.

I was always moved by the ancient story of Diwali, which tells of the triumph of good over evil. That story made me want to be good and kind and heroic myself.

Maybe this is why Dad bought those fireworks each year — to teach me to keep Diwali in my heart, always.

NOTE FROM NIDHI CHANANI

Diwali is my favorite holiday of the year. Even though my family was part of a large Indian community in Los Angeles, my neighbors and schoolmates were not Indian. Therefore on our street, we celebrated alone. My mom made special food, I received new clothes, we lit sparklers, and we called my mom's family in India to wish them a happy Diwali. Each ritual left an impression but most of all I remember the lights. The stainless-steel plate full of lit *diyas* in the darkness. We placed a *diya* in each room of our home. Outside, we set them in a row leading to the front door. As the only home on our street with *diyas*, I recall looking up at the stars and thinking that thousands of miles away, the other half of my family was celebrating too. I imagined the trail of bright lights connecting us across the globe. Even now when I light *diyas* I think of this and it's why I will always love Diwali.

For Dav and Sayuri,
who spread light wherever they go.
— T.U.

For my brilliant Chanani family, who taught me to love Diwali,
and my Giordano family that shines a light in my life.
— N.C.

Library of Congress Cataloging-in-Publication Data available
ISBN 978-1-338-36448-4

10 9 8 7 6 5 22 23 24 25 26
Printed in China 38
First edition, September 2020

The illustrations were created digitally with handmade texture brushes.
Book design by Charles Kreloff